CODE 900

A Derrick Stone Crime Story

by
Kenn Crawford

CRAWFORD HOUSE PUBLISHING
GLACE BAY, NOVA SCOTIA, CANADA

Copyright © 2020 Kenn Crawford

THANK YOU FOR SUPPORTING
INDEPENDENT WRITERS

ISBN: 978-1-989911-03-7

This is a work of fiction. Names, characters, events and incidents are the products of the author's imagination. Any resemblance to actual persons, living or dead, or events, is purely coincidental. The opinions expressed are those of the characters and should not be confused with those of the author.

About the Author

Born in Toronto in 1966, Kenn Crawford grew up in the coal mining town of Glace Bay on Cape Breton – an island off the coast of Nova Scotia, Canada.

 Kenn spent his childhood reading books and making up stories; a hobby that led to his love of writing poetry, songs and short stories. Eventually he began writing books and screenplays.

He wrote a weekly newspaper column about songwriting and home recording, and was showcased in *The Cape Bretoner Magazine* as the featured songwriter.

In 2016, he took his love of making up stories to the next level by writing, shooting and directing short films.

In 2018, he won a *Canada Shorts* Director's Award of Commendation.

Kenn lives in his hometown of Glace Bay with his fiancé, Margie, shooting short films and music videos, and teaching writing and filmmaking workshops. He is currently working on several new fiction and nonfiction books.

For more information about Kenn, his writing and his film work, visit his website at: **www.kenncrawford.com**

Books by Kenn Crawford

Dead Hunt

The Saga of Bayou Billy

The Misadventures of Mallory Malo

The Covid Chronicles

The Princess Knights

Code 900

for Derrick

I wanted you to see what real courage is, instead of getting the idea that courage is a man with a gun in his hand.

~Harper Lee, To Kill a Mockingbird

Prologue

A SLATE grey sky blanketed the ancient tombstones in muted hues. Deep shadows slithered across the skeletons of fallen leaves like a silent predator stalking its prey. Naked trees that once sheltered the long-forgotten burial ground stood drowsing as morning's first light struggled against the gloomy haze.

Ashen, crumbling leaves carpeted the forgotten cemetery as heavy, black police shoes blemished the serene, earthen floor.

A bundle was dropped effortlessly with a sickening thud. Blood dripped from the rolled-up carpet and painted the withering leaves in crimson. A small shovel bit into the consecrated ground. The sound of metal scraping against rock disturbed the morning calm.

A mouthful of silence hung in the air when the blood-soaked carpet twitched. A groan sounded from within, breaking the deafening quiet. Seconds later, the bundle moved hysterically as a woman's head broke free from its cocoon.

Her eyes, wet with fear and confusion, glared with hate as she recognized her assailant. Her blood simultaneously chilled and boiled as the metal blade of the raised shovel glistened briefly in the growing light.

A scream punctuated the crushing blow.

Derrick

NINE MONTHS EARLIER…

THE CONFEDERATION Ferry rocked rhythmically as it swallowed the last of the passenger cars in preparation of its crossing from Caribou, Nova Scotia to Wood Islands, located on Prince Edward Island.

Police Cadet Derrick Stone turned his collar to the cold, damp breeze as he walked across the deck to wave goodbye to family and friends who made the two-hour drive from Glace Bay to bid him farewell.

A few were high school friends, but most were fellow students and sparring partners from Bailey's Martial Arts Academy where Derrick spent his free time studying, and often teaching, self-defence.

They all knew of Derrick's life-long goal, and they were excited that he was accepted into the Maritime Police Academy.

As the ferry cast off and rocked its way towards Wood Islands, Derrick found his way to the lounge area to meet up with his fellow cadets. Standing six foot one and weighing in at two hundred and five pounds, Derrick Stone was the second-largest cadet aboard the Confederation.

P.A.R.E.

AT SIX foot eight and topping the scales at two hundred and eighty pounds, James McElroy, 'Big Jim' as he was known to family and friends, held the honour of being the biggest cadet in the Academy's forty-year history.

The two behemoths first met a month earlier at the Academy during the P.A.R.E. test, the Physical Abilities Requirement Exercises. Both men passed the excruciating test, and just like every cadet before them, they both quickly vomited when they crossed the finish line of the exhausting and muscle-taxing obstacle course.

Derrick successfully completed his first test in just under the required four minutes, but when he crossed the finish line carrying the eighty-pound dummy, he triumphantly slammed it to the ground much like a footballer slams the pigskin after a touchdown.

Penalized for not properly laying the torso down, Derrick was forced to repeat the gruelling obstacle course.

When Derrick successfully completed it for the second time, he gently laid the torso down as if placing a sleeping baby in its cradle. When the drill instructor announced that Derrick had successfully passed the test, he playfully kicked the dummy, then was promptly reprimanded for his efforts.

Big Jim failed the course on his first attempt but squeaked out a pass on his second try. Most cadets failed their first attempt while some never made it. The only cadet to pass the course on their first attempt, not counting Derrick's unofficial pass before he slammed the dummy's torso to the ground, was female cadet, Josephine "Jo" MacDonald.

The Ladies

ABOARD THE Confederation Ferry, Jo sat with her back to the wall and scanned the room robotically. From behind her non-prescription glasses, her fawn-like eyes never stopped for more than a few seconds on any one thing or person. Her naturally blonde hair, pulled back in a functional ponytail, was dyed a deep black. Jo did not wear makeup, she didn't need to, and preferred ball caps to tiaras. Despite her attempts of looking plain and unattractive in oversized clothes, her natural beauty could not be contained.

Seated next to Jo was the only other female cadet, Amanda "Mandy" Smith. Strawberry blonde hair hung to Mandy's shoulders, her full lips glistening in layers of pink lip gloss. Unlike Jo, Mandy did not try to hide her good looks.

Raised by religious zealots, Mandy spent her teenage years buried beneath layers of clothing, even during record-breaking summer temperatures. Family outings to the beach were an exercise in humiliation and constant taunting from her peers. On her eighteenth birthday, Mandy escaped her parent's domineering influence by setting off on her own.

Her inhibitions, and several layers of clothing, were quickly cast aside. Yet despite her whimsical, carefree attitude and mannerisms more reminiscent of a dumb party girl, Mandy passed the P.S.T., the Police Science Test, with relative ease.

Designed not to be completed, Derrick and Mandy were the only two cadets to finish the entire P.S.T. test in the allotted time, with Mandy etching out the highest score by a mere three points.

Clay

THE CADETS were joined in the lounge by the only other person from Cape Breton Island, Clay Lake. Sporting his trademark FBI ball cap, Clay left his First Nations reservation on a personal quest.

Between the ages of thirteen and fifteen, he was arrested repeatedly for minor offences, mostly drunk and disorderly conduct and fighting. At nineteen he had already fathered two children. Clay buried his oldest girl before her second birthday, the victim of a drunk driver speeding through the reservation.

As each shovel-full of dirt was thrown on his daughter's tiny casket, Clay vowed that no parent on the Rez would ever have to bury their children – not on his watch.

The Trans-Canada highway cut through the middle of the Reservation; speeding cars were a common sight as motorists hurried along with little respect for the speed limit. Many a dog, and the occasional child, were struck down by speeding cars.

After his daughter's funeral, Clay replaced the official speed limit signs with crudely made versions that warned drivers to slow down. He set up improvised roadblocks to slow traffic and gave unofficial roadside sobriety tests.

Clay had even made several citizen's arrests of drunk drivers and handcuffed them to their steering wheels until the RCMP, the Royal Canadian Mounted Police, had arrived on the Rez to arrest and charge the drunk drivers.

Despite his good intentions, the RCMP suffered constant complaints from weary travellers who had to endure Clay's relentless patrols and roadblocks.

Impressed by his actions and dedication to making his community safer, albeit a little perturbed that he often made them look bad by catching more drunk drivers than they did, they offered to put Clay through RCMP training to officially make him an officer of the law.

But when Clay discovered that an RCMP Constable was not allowed to patrol in their hometown, or in Clay's case, on the Rez, Clay declined their offer and applied for a student loan to attend the Maritime Police Academy.

With no collateral to secure a loan, and a criminal record marring his honourable intentions, Clay was denied financial support. Members of his community held several local fundraisers and even started a GoFundMe campaign.

Word of how a distraught father was fighting back to prevent the senseless killings of young children on the Rez was first picked up by local newspapers, then went national across the country. The outpouring of support to help Clay raised the twenty-seven thousand dollars needed for tuition, books and policing equipment.

Clay amended his vow to include studying and working his ass off to not let his good Samaritans down by being the best police officer he could be.

The Academy

"WELCOME TO the Maritime Police Academy," Officer Wilson welcomed the group. "For the next thirty-five weeks, we own your ass."

Most of the cadets fidgeted nervously. Derrick bit back a smile trying not to look too enthusiastic. Clay yawned in boredom.

"Lake, MacDonald, McElroy, Smith and Stone, you'll join Slade with your instructor, Sergeant Burke. Squad Thirty-Five."

A man with bulging arms and thick shoulders stepped forward.

"Good morning, boys and girls," Sergeant Burke said looking at the five cadets, "Everyone else arrived at the scheduled eleven hundred hours. You're late. I know your boat got delayed due to rough seas, so today you get your one and only *Get Out of Jail Free Card."*

"The next time you're late," Burke added, "you'll pay dearly."

Clay yawned again.

Derrick smiled, eager to get started.

The Big Brawl

THE WEEKS that followed found the squads competing against each other, and themselves. The cadets were granted permission to go home for the weekend, with strict orders to report back at the academy on Sunday morning by eleven hundred hours.

Most of the cadets headed back to Nova Scotia and New Brunswick to visit their families and loved ones, but Derrick, Mandy and Jo stayed on the island. Mandy spent her weekends exploring the island, which usually meant a party somewhere in Charlottetown, and Jo sequestered herself to her room studying.

Derrick asked permission to ride shotgun with the island's Provincial Police, and eagerly signed a waiver stating that if he was hurt while on patrol and unable to finish training, he would have to reapply the following year. Despite the risk of possibly losing his spot, and his tuition, Derrick gave up his weekend furlough for a chance to get on-the-job training.

On patrol, he felt like an actual cop instead of a cadet, and he wore his uniform with pride. His sleeves still bore the Maritime Police Academy patch, but the rest of the uniform was identical to a regular officer's uniform from the cap down to his black police boots. The only thing missing on his uniform was a gun holster... and the gun.

The last call of Derrick's first shift was to break up a large brawl at a Charlottetown nightclub. Armed with only a flashlight and a pair of handcuffs, Derrick was ordered to keep his back to his partner until backup arrived.

"If anyone comes at you," the officer explained, "knock him the fuck out!"

Derrick couldn't help but smile when he thought, *I am so gonna like this job.*

Standing in a defensive position, hands raised in a boxer's stance with his left hand tightly gripping his long flashlight, Derrick silently wished someone would be dumb enough to take a swing at him. It wasn't long before an overzealous and cocky drunk answered his prayer.

The drunk smirked at the unarmed cadet as he dropped a ball from the pool table into a sock and swung it like a mace as he stepped towards the officers. Derrick, smiling, leaned forward, taunting the man to attack. The man swung and Derrick easily dodged the socked weapon and delivered a right cross flush into the man's face. Three of the man's teeth flew across the room as his legs buckled. He was unconscious before he even hit the floor.

Another attacker rushed to his drunken friend's aid while swinging a broken cue stick. Derrick blocked the blow with his flashlight. That man felt the knuckles of Derrick's fist as it crushed his nose. He too was asleep when he bounced off the floor.

When the backup arrived with guns drawn, the fighting was brought to a sudden halt.

I am so gonna like this job, Derrick thought again as he tried not to smile too much.

"Stone," the cop he was riding with yelled to him. "Next time there's a brawl, try not to get a woody when you're knocking people out."

Derrick flushed red.

"Oh, and Stone," the officer added as he placed his hand on Derrick's shoulder, "you can ride with me anytime, son."

Derrick smiled.

Yeah, I'm really gonna like this job, Derrick thought as the officer dropped him off at the Academy.

As he watched the patrol car pull away, Derrick spotted Mandy staggering towards the dorms. He shook his head in disapproval.

Mandy

MANDY STUMBLED into her dorm room and promptly collapsed on her bed. She kept one foot on the floor to try and keep the room from spinning. It didn't work. A sudden knock at her door broke the silence.

Reluctantly she stood on wobbly legs and focused on keeping her eyes open. Steadying herself with anything she could grab a hold of for balance, she staggered to the door and lethargically opened it. For her efforts, she was greeted by a fist to the face.

Mandy flew backwards and crashed to the hard floor. Adrenaline chased her drunkenness away. She tried to scramble to her feet but was kicked in her abdomen, knocking the wind out of her.

She gasped for air in a silent scream as the assailant's fist crashed into her temple. Her equilibrium now completely thrown off balance, Mandy struggled to fight off unconsciousness. Her blurred, teary-eyed vision saw only the bottom of a black boot just before it stomped her into unconsciousness.

As the morning classes began, the cadets were informed that S.W.A.T. was visiting the academy to train the Island's police officers, and the cadets were invited to attend the demonstrations. Every cadet attended the S.W.A.T. classes except Mandy, who was recovering from injuries she claimed to have received from falling down a flight of stairs, and Jo, who sat vigil by her side.

"When we are on the job," Jo tried to convince Mandy, "we're supposed to convince women to testify and tell the truth about what happened."

"We're not on the job," Mandy reminded her as a tear escaped and trickled down her bruised cheek.

"Besides, we both know the burden of proof lies with the woman, but I can't remember anything. I barely remember opening the door. I didn't see anything, so I don't have any proof."

"I'm looking at all the proof I need," Jo said as she gently stroked Mandy's swollen cheek.

Self-Defence

THE FOLLOWING week the cadets were informed the regular self-defence instructor had to leave on a family emergency. Most of the cadets expected a new instructor, a couple hoped for the afternoon off. All were surprised when Sergeant Wilson asked Derrick to teach the class.

"Are you kidding me?" Big Jim snarled, "We're supposed to learn how to fight from another cadet?"

The Sergeant smiled knowingly and invited Big Jim to the mat. He presented Jim a rubber knife and told him to attack Derrick. A few seconds later, Big Jim was looking up at the ceiling wondering how he landed on his back.

Derrick smiled and tossed the rubber knife back to Jim. As

Derrick started to explain the finer points of disarming an attacker, Big Jim feinted with the knife and threw a vicious left hook.

The last thing Big Jim remembered, right before he felt his legs crumble beneath him, was Derrick's elbow smashing into his face.

When Big Jim regained consciousness, he apologized to Derrick and asked him to teach him self-defence… only this time, without knocking him out.

The Beach

CLAY SPENT every other weekend back home in Cape Breton with his daughter, other weekends he spent on campus studying to make sure he graduated. He often cleared his head by taking walks along Prince Edward Island's long, sandy beaches. He carried his black, academy-issued shoes draped over his shoulder and he let the red clay sand of Prince Edward Island ooze between his toes.

Mandy walked alongside him carrying a small, pink plastic bucket. They collected seashells and found a starfish to bring back home to his daughter. He watched children playing on the beach and a pang of homesickness stabbed at his heart.

"You must really miss your daughter?" Mandy asked, more of a statement than a question.

"More than you know," Clay answered, still watching the children play.

Mandy silently wished she had known him in a different life; one where he wasn't married. She knew there was so much more to him than the bad-boy reputation he worked so hard to maintain.

I guess, Mandy thought, *being anything but a badass is a sign of weakness on his reservation*. Mandy had to admit that she knew nothing of his people or his culture; she was only guessing and daydreaming. Even when he looked away, she continued to stare at his strong features. She knew that beneath his rough and crude exterior lived a gentle creature. Mandy playfully kicked water at Clay and raced down the beach.

When Clay caught up to her, he lifted her in his arms and threatened to throw her in the ocean. Mandy wiggled and squirmed helplessly. When he reached the shoreline, she tried desperately to free herself and accidentally slammed her elbow into his nose. Clay eased her down and wiped a small trickle of blood with the back of his hand.

"Oh my god," Mandy apologized, almost in tears, "I am so, so sorry. I didn't mean to---"

"Damn girl," Clay smiled, "I knew you were a heart breaker, but I didn't think my nose was in jeopardy too."

She punched him playfully in the arm.

"Serves you right, trying to throw me in the water."

"No harm, no foul," he said with a wink. "Next time I'll just have to remember to duck."

Mandy flexed her arm. "I'm tougher than I look, big boy."

Clay touched his nose. "No kidding."

As Mandy nursed his nose to stop the bleeding, she noticed a sudden seriousness overcome him.

"What's wrong?" She asked.

"Mandy," Clay answered, "can I ask you a… well… a personal question?"

Mandy looked into his deep brown eyes. She smiled warmly, not sure where the conversation was headed.

"Sure, Clay."

"What really happened? You know… when you were… umm, hurt?"

Mandy released her breath slowly as her mind drifted back to that night.

"To be honest, I'm not really sure. I had a few drinks." She paused, then amended her statement. "A few too many actually. I remember a knock at my door, but when I opened it I was greeted by a punch in the face. I don't think I would have been able to stop it even if I was sober. Christ, it happened so fast. I don't remember much after that, other than getting the shit kicked out of me before I passed out."

"Were you… you know…?" Clay looked embarrassed but genuinely concerned.

"Raped?" Mandy finished his question. "No, I don't think I was."

"You don't think? Didn't you go to the hospital and get checked out?"

"No. If I was, I would… well… I would know. I wasn't. I was just beat up."

"But why?"

Mandy snorted a laugh. "Well that's the sixty-four-thousand-dollar question, isn't it? If I knew why then maybe I would know who did it."

"Doesn't make sense," Clay thought out loud. "To have something like that happen at the academy and nothing was done about it."

"Nothing was done because nobody knows. Well, nobody but Jo, and now you, know what really happened. And that's the way I want to keep it."

Clay shook his head, "Why keep it a secret? Somebody needs to pay."

"Somebody did pay."

Clay looked at her, confused.

"I paid. I was the party girl. I work my ass off all week to be a cop and then I let loose and party too hard on the weekend. I threw caution to the wind and just looked forward to a good time. Well, constantly partying has a price, and I paid it. But the price could have been a lot worse."

"Yeah," Clay answered, "It could have been a lot worse."

"In a twisted sort of way," Mandy explained, "whoever did that to me taught me a valuable lesson I won't soon forget. I'm just glad Jo checked in on me and found me."

Clay placed his arm around her, and Mandy leaned into him as they walked along the beach.

"It just pisses me off," Clay said, "that a cadet got away with hurting you. We're supposed to be cops for Christ's sake, not thugs."

"Who said it was one of us?" Mandy answered. "We don't know that. The academy is pretty big with a lot of people coming and going on the weekends. It could have been anyone."

"True," Clay sighed.

"Hey, Tonto," a voice sounded, interrupting their conversation. Clay turned to see three locals, beer bottles in hand, walking towards them. "Would you look at that, he's wearing an FBI hat," the first man taunted. "Don't you know the FBI don't take red skins?"

Clay quickly moved Mandy behind him as the biggest of the

three men stepped closer.

"We don't want your kind here," the man slurred, "so why don't you fuck off back to your backwoods reservation. And don't worry about that sweet piece of ass you got there," the man said grabbing his crotch, "me and the boys here will take real good care of her."

The man poked a finger in Clay's chest. "Now run along Chief, before I bitch slap you."

Bad idea, Mandy thought as she took a few steps back, *Very bad idea.*

Clay yawned. "Is this the part where I get scared, or does that come later?"

"What the fuck did you say to me?" The man snarled.

"Well," Clay smiled, "I know you're working really, really hard at intimidating me, so I don't want to be rude and miss the part where I'm supposed to be scared."

"You some kinda tough guy?" The man slurred as he poked Clay's chest again.

Clay grabbed the man's wrist with one hand and the finger that poked him with his other hand and snapped it backwards. The man's shriek of pain drowned out the sound of cracking bones.

The other two men rushed in. Clay planted his feet and met the onslaught with a vicious overhand right. The man in front crumpled from the impact as Clay raised his left to block the punch from the third man.

Clay grabbed him by the throat and squeezed, blocking his air. The man struggled to grab Clay's wrists to free himself, but Clay kneed him in the groin. The man's shriek of agony punctuated the end of their brief attack. The three men writhed in pain on the wet sand.

Clay reached back for Mandy's hand. She took it willingly.

Clay leaned down to the first man who was still whimpering and whispered, "Just so you know shithead, FBI stands for Fucking Big Indian."

Mandy smiled and squeezed Clay's hand as they continued their walk along the beach.

The Club

BIG JIM spent his weekends back in Glace Bay with his fiancée, Susan, a waitress at *The Old 42 Bar & Grill* where he worked as a bouncer before joining the academy. For months, Big Jim had watched and protected Susan and the other waitresses from drunk patrons who got a little too friendly and tried to grope the girls.

At first, Big Jim would handle the altercations rather peacefully, but as his feelings for Susan grew, and their relationship blossomed, Big Jim became more violent towards the men who tried to grab her the wrong way.

Knowing of his desire to be a police officer, the club owner tried to overlook Jim's jealous fits, and always backed his story whenever Jim was questioned by the police because he hospitalized someone.

Everyone, Susan included, was glad when Big Jim finally got accepted to the academy so he would be spending most of his time off the island and away from the club.

Susan loved the sweet and tender side of Big Jim that most people rarely got a chance to see, but ever since they started dating, her tips were on a steady decline, and tension between them started to grow.

Susan managed to get every Saturday off so she and Big Jim could spend some quality time together, away from the club, when he came home for a visit. The club was short-staffed and needed her to work, but the owner knew it was for the best; the last thing any of them needed was a jealous monster cracking heads again.

The last thing Big Jim needed was to get arrested while training to be a cop.

Batter Up

SIX HOURS away, in a part of Halifax that doesn't get promoted on the city's tourist brochures, Slade pulled his '67 Mustang into the parking lot of an abandoned warehouse and lit a cigarette. Five minutes later, a black van rolled to a stop next to him. Slade crushed the cigarette on the heel of his boot and strolled over to the driver's window.

"Did you get a name for me?" Slade asked.

The driver looked around the parking lot nervously, "I heard me an ugly rumour 'bout you." He said as his eyes darted from side to side.

"Yeah? And what would that be?" Slade asked.

"That you joined up with the pigs."

Slade laughed. "Keep your friends close and your enemies closer."

"What's that s'pposed to mean?"

"It means shut the fuck up," Slade answered, "or I'll kick your black ass all over this parking lot."

"Why you gots to be so mean, Slade? I was just axin' man."

"You don't ask shit unless I tell you what questions to 'axe' you illiterate piece of shit. Now did you get me the guy's fuckin' name or not?"

"Yeah, I got it," The driver said as beads of sweat glistened his forehead. "Yer sister's been meetin' up with Little Joe over at the motel on---"

"Little Joe!" Slade said, interrupting. "Little fuckin' Joe? Are you gonna sit there and tell me that lazy fuckin' Indian is bangin' my little sister?"

The man raised his hands defensively, "I ain't sayin' nuttin' Slade, I'm just tellin' ya what you axed me to git."

"Are they there now?"

Another onslaught of nervous sweat beaded on the driver's forehead. He nodded sullenly. Slade punched the side of the van, rage streaming through his veins.

Slade retrieved an aluminum baseball bat from the trunk of his car and got in the passenger side of the van.

"Time for a little baseball," Slade said as he closed the door, "I hear the Indians are about to strike out."

Shotgun

THE LAST weekend before graduation, Derrick was riding shotgun with the Provincial Police when the radio squawked for them to respond to a domestic violence call. Derrick learned that during such calls to always place something between him and the suspects, and to never turn your back to the women being abused.

Too many times the victim attacked the officer to prevent their husband or boyfriend from being arrested. Officers have been hit with everything from brooms to frying pans while others have been stabbed by the person they were trying to protect.

"Let me do the talking, you just stay behind me and watch my back," the officer had instructed Derrick.

When they entered the premises, the suspect was seated on the couch drinking from a bottle of Jack Daniels, his feet up on the coffee table. The victim lay in the corner curled up in a fetal position.

It wasn't a wife or girlfriend that was beaten, this was the man's nine-year-old daughter. Her arms were covered in bruises, some new, some several days old. Tears streamed from her swollen eyes; cuts from the man's ring disfigured her pretty face as blood from between her legs stained her soiled underwear.

"Sir," the officer said, thinking of his own daughter and fighting the urge to just shoot the man. "Stand up. You're coming with us."

"Go fuck yourself, pig!" the man laughed as he took another swallow of Jack Daniels. The officer took a step back and looked at Derrick, "Well, I'm done talking. Your turn."

Derrick looked at the little girl then at the man. Disgust and hatred boiled in his veins. He stepped forward, grabbed the coffee table and fired it across the room. It shattered against the wall.

"You were told to get on your feet!" Derrick ordered.

"And you were told to go fuck yourself!" The man said with a cocky grin as he lifted the bottle for another drink. Derrick grabbed the bottle from the man's hand and fired it against the wall; his other hand grabbed the man by the face and lifted him off the couch. The other officer wrapped the young girl in a blanket and carried her outside.

When he returned to the house, the man was laying on the floor, barely conscious, blood poured from his face.

"What happened?" The officer asked Derrick.

"He fell down," Derrick answered.

"Guess he shouldn't of been drinking so much," the officer replied as he cuffed the man and dragged him to his feet.

Derrick watched as the officer mysteriously lost his grip and the man fell face first down the concrete front steps.

When backup arrived on the scene, the officer with Derrick told them to first look at the young girl sitting in the back of his cruiser before saying anything. Once they saw the condition the young girl was in, no one seemed to notice the man's battered face.

When Child Protective Services and an ambulance arrived, the girl was transferred to the ambulance and the father was thrown into the back of the cruiser.

"This is not what we are about," the officer explained to Derrick, "but I suggest you put your seatbelt on."

Derrick snapped his seatbelt closed as the officer accelerated.

They sped down the highway, lights flashing, as the cuffed man spewed insults and threats at them.

"Do you see that cat?' the officer asked.

"What cat?' Derrick started to answer as the officer slammed on the brakes.

Derrick's seatbelt dug into his shoulder as the man flew forward, his face slamming into the protective screen that separated the prisoners from the officers.

"You just witnessed your first screening," the officer said as he pulled the car over to the side of the road. Derrick said nothing as the officer dragged the man from the car to check his injuries.

"Stop struggling," the officer ordered mockingly as he dug his knee into the man's back and pushed hard on the back of the man's head, forcing the man's face into the asphalt.

"You better call this in," the officer said to Derrick, "he tried to escape and is resisting arrest."

The officer placed his knee on the back of the man's head and put his full weight into it. Screams of pain and profanity quickly followed.

The official report stated that the man received injuries when the car had to make an emergency stop. It also stated the man's primary injuries were the result of him falling down the stairs in a drunken state. Additional injuries were the result of him trying to escape and resisting arrest.

Knowing what that pitiful excuse of a man did to that little girl, no one seemed interested in following up with the report.

Graduation Day

DURING THE graduation ceremony, Derrick thought about that young girl. *There's a lot of things I'm not going to like about this job,* Derrick thought as he was given his badge.

"Now that you're training is done," Sergeant Wilson explained, "a group of officers and detectives from Cape Breton are hosting a special demonstration on I-DENT and Murder Investigations. It's a weekend course, and it's strictly volunteer. I know some of you wish to return to your families and celebrate, but I urge each of you to consider taking this invaluable course. It will be squad Thirty-Five against squad Thirty-Six. Anyone interested?"

"Hell yeah!" one of them roared. "Let's show them what we are made of!"

Cheers followed as Sergeant Wilson produced two sealed envelopes.

"Stone," the Sergeant explained as he handed Derrick the first envelope, "You're Team Leader for Squad Thirty-five. Barlow, you're Squad Leader for Thirty-Six. Each of you holds a map for the first leg of this exercise. Think of it as a cross between a scavenger hunt and a crime scene investigation.

"Each team has a designated vehicle parked somewhere on this island. When you find your vehicle, you will be given directions for an area somewhere on Cape Breton where you will discover a mock crime scene. You must secure the area and collect evidence.

"The name of the game is: *Solve the Crime*. The first team to successfully break the case within forty-eight hours wins."

"What's the prize, Sarge?" Barlow asked.

"My undying admiration."

Everyone chuckled.

"It's not about winning a prize, it's about" the Sergeant smiled, then amended his statement. "Okay, it is about winning a prize."

Everyone chuckled.

"The Academy," the sergeant explained, "will send the first team to solve the case on a week-long vacation to beautiful Punta Cana."

They nodded, approvingly.

"Remember boys and girls," the sergeant reminded them, "this exercise is our way of finding out who has what it takes to be a detective. So it's not all fun and games. Each of you will be evaluated on individual and team performance. Good luck."

"Any inside tips?" One of the officers asked.

The Sergeant smiled, "Just one: the clock's ticking, so don't waste time asking stupid questions."

Squad thirty-five huddled closely as Derrick opened the envelope. In it was a crudely hand-drawn map with a red X and a set of keys.

"What in the hell is this supposed to mean?" Slade asked as he yanked the paper from Derrick's hand. "I know three-year-olds that can draw better than this. How are we supposed to use this? It doesn't even make sense."

"That's the point, dumb ass," Jo said as she pulled the map from Slade's hand and flattened it on the hood of a police cruiser. On the map were crudely little squares designating buildings. Jo scanned the campus and quickly decided it was not a representation of the Police Academy.

"So where is it?" Jo asked, looking at Derrick.

"How in the hell am I supposed to know?"

"Well, you're the one who went cruising all over the island every weekend riding shotgun with the locals. Surely something must look familiar?"

Derrick studied the map then smiled. He reached into the glove box and retrieved a map of Prince Edward Island.

"Here," he said, pointing to the hand-drawn map. Look at the way the wavy lines run into the road." They all stared blankly at the hand-drawn map.

"It's water," he explained, "and a bridge. So all we have to do is find a place on this map with a similar layout."

"Maps don't show buildings," Slade announced.

"Actually," Mandy said, "they do. Look." She pointed at the map. Police stations, churches, libraries, fire stations, hospitals, they're all marked. This building here on the hand-drawn map has a plus sign so it's either a church or a hospital."

"Well that narrows it down," Slade snorted sarcastically.

"If you're not going to say something constructive," Big Jim cautioned, "just shut up and let the grownups figure this out."

"Let's start by looking at towns near the water with bridges," Derrick suggested.

"Near the water?" Slade laughed, "Are you serious? We're on a fuckin' island."

"Can we trade him to another team?" Clay asked as he pushed Slade aside and pointed to the map.

"Look here," he said pointing to the map of Prince Edward Island, "This town right here has a harbour and a bridge, and up here is a hospital. If these lines on the hand-drawn map are roads, they match up pretty damn close to the town of Montague."

"Works for me," Derrick said. "So the next question is: how do we get to Montague?"

Slade tapped the hood of the car, "They didn't say anything about *not* borrowing academy property."

They all smiled.

"And our first official job as new police officers," Mandy laughed, "is stealing a couple of police cruisers. I like it."

"Me too, and I'm driving," Slade said with a huge grin.

"Now we get to see what we're really made of," Jo said as she playfully elbowed Derrick.

Thirty-five minutes later they found a black van parked in front of the Montague convenience store with two police officers standing next to it.

"I'm Officer Roberts," the female officer introduced herself. "I see you took a few liberties and borrowed a couple of cruisers."

Slade smiled as Squad Thirty-Five gathered around them.

"I'm impressed, you guys got here pretty fast," Roberts said as her partner handed her a yellow, manila envelope. "We expected to be here for at least a few more hours."

"That's why we're the best, sweet thing," Slade smiled as his eyes explored her curves. "And speaking of the best, anytime you want to spend a night with the best---"

"Here are your instructions," Roberts said as she shoved the envelope at him. "There's a map and some cash to cover expenses." She glared at Slade. "Use it wisely. All cell phones and radios are to be left with us. You'll be camping out in the beautiful Margaree on Cape Breton Island."

"We wouldn't happen to be camping in a motel, would we?' Mandy smiled.

"Actually," Roberts said with a sly grin. "you'll be camping in the mountains that surround Margaree. Your campsite is marked on the map. Tents and sleeping bags are in the van."

Mandy groaned. "So we're not just camping in the middle of nowhere, it's the middle of nowhere on top of a mountain. Great."

"Look on the bright side, I hear the autumn colours are amazing," Officer Roberts smiled. Tomorrow, you will discover a mock murder. You are not to seek outside help under any circumstances. The idea of this training exercise is to be completely cut off with…" She glared at Slade again, "with only each other. So…secure the scene, gather evidence, and crack the case within forty-eight hours. Good luck."

Squad Thirty-Five waved goodbye and piled into the van.

Slade gunned the engine. Destination: The Wood Islands Ferry.

Cape Breton Island

AS THE Confederation Ferry docked in Caribou, Nova Scotia, Derrick and his team had already formulated a dozen possible scenarios and what clues to look for. Derrick and Mandy led the conversation while Slade drove. As he sped down the Trans-Canada Highway towards Cape Breton, flashing red and blue lights made Slade look at the speedometer. He was doing 120km in an eighty zone.

"I told you to slow the fuck down," Clay said as the van rolled to a stop.

"Bite me, Chief," Slade replied as he rolled the window down.

The cop looked at Slade then the passengers. They were all dressed in identical Police Academy sweats but the officer never seemed to notice.

"License and registration please?"

Slade looked at the others and cocked his eyebrow. In unison, they all pulled out their badges.

The cop shook his head, "You'd think that a van with this many cops would have enough sense to obey the speed limit."

Slade smiled, "Sorry officer, Chief back there is the cautious driver, I'm---"

"An asshole," Clay said as he threatened to slap the back of Slade's head.

"Okay boys, play nice... and slow down!" The officer ordered.

"Yes, sir," Slade said with a salute.

The cop shook his head and walked back to his car.

When the taillights of the cruiser disappeared, Slade looked at the others and smiled.

"We're near Havre Boucher, about fifteen minutes or so from the Canso Causeway. Twenty bucks says I can pass that cruiser and make it across the Causeway without getting caught."

Derrick laughed. "Fifty bucks says Clay kicks your ass if you don't slow down."

Slade grunted, "Bunch of candy asses."

An hour and a half later the van pulled into the parking lot of *The Red Barn Gift Shop and Restaurant* just outside the village of Baddeck, a popular tourist attraction and home to Alexander Graham Bell.

"Might as well grab some breakfast," Slade suggested. "It could be a couple of days before we see real food again."

They piled out of the van and headed for the restaurant. They found a table big enough to accommodate all of them and placed their orders.

They all ordered bacon and eggs with home fries; all except Mandy. She ordered a monstrous stack of French Toast. She smothered it in butter, drizzled them with a thick layer of maple syrup, then artfully dusted it with a generous sprinkling of powdered sugar.

She dug in. Ecstasy.

Mandy wiped her lips and looked at her fellow officers staring at her.

"What?" She asked as she sipped her coffee.

"How can someone as skinny as you eat that much food?" Clay asked playfully.

"I have a high metabolism." Mandy smiled as she shoved another forkful of pancakes into her mouth.

Jo pretended to push her plate away, "I'm full just watching her eat."

They all laughed and finished their meals in relative silence.

Margaree

THE VAN pulled into the designated campsite at noon. The site wasn't an actual campsite, it was little more than a barren field located on one of the mountains that surrounded Margaree Valley.

"I remember this place," Jo announced to her fellow officers. "My family use to rent a cottage near here when I was a kid. We told each other ghost stories of how that old house over there was haunted. I think there's a hunting blind down the hill on the other side of that clearing."

They all scanned their surroundings, taking in the natural beauty of the place. The dilapidated house was faded grey with time; nature had reclaimed it as trees jutted up through the broken roof. Black, glassless windows gave the old building an ominous, uninviting look.

"We need to make sure we wear the Hunter's Orange vests at all times," Derrick suggested. "It's fall, and even though hunting season hasn't officially started yet, there may be a few poachers trying to get a head start. So let's not go anywhere without a vest on."

"Yes, dad," Slade answered sarcastically.

"Pale skin speak truth," Clay offered in an exaggerated accent, "crazy white man always shoot anything that moves."

They all laughed then started to unload their camping gear.

"So where should we set up?" Jo asked.

"I'm thinking right where we are standing is good," Derrick suggested.

"Next to the creepy, old house," Mandy smiled, "wonderful."

"Then why not camp down in the clearing?" Slade asked.

"Because that's where the deer will be," Jo informed him. "If a hunter starts shooting, we don't want to be in his line of fire."

Slade laughed and drew his pistol. He spun it around his finger like a cowboy from an old western movie.

"No worries, we're all armed," Slade said, grinning.

Mandy patted him on the shoulder, "Guns shoot bullets genius, they don't stop them."

Slade smiled, red-faced, as he returned his gun to its holster.

An hour later, the tents were set up and a small campfire was crackling. Slade unloaded the case of beer the academy was kind enough to leave for them. He offered a can to everyone. Mandy refused. Slade just shrugged.

"More for me. What about you, Chief?" Slade asked.

Clay shook his head.

"What's the matter, you too good to drink with us?"

"I don't drink," Clay answered with a calm smile.

"One beer ain't gonna hurt you, Chief."

"Lay off, Slade," Derrick said as he popped his can of beer open. "He has his reasons."

"Maybe he's afraid he'll get drunk and go all native on us," Slade laughed.

Clay stood up abruptly, his calm demeanor all but gone.

Slade jumped to his feet, fists clenched.

"What? You got something to say to me, Chief?"

"That's enough!" Mandy said as she stepped between them, a hand on each of their chests. "We don't need your testosterone screwing up our chances of winning this competition."

The two men eyed each other in silence.

"You better listen to your bitch… Chief," Slade taunted Clay.

Clay yawned, bored, and sat back down.

"That's right. Sit yer ass down, Injun."

Big Jim stepped in front of Slade, looking down at him.

"You sit YOUR ass down." Big Jim ordered.

Slade hesitated, then thought better of it and sat down, cracking open a beer.

"You're all a bunch of fuckin' pussies," Slade said between mouthfuls of beer. "Can't even take a joke."

"Nobody's laughing but you," Derrick answered.

The fire danced and cracked into the night as the sun fell behind the mountains and the team drifted into slumber.

The hungry and relentless darkness swallowed the camp as the last of the burning embers turned to ash.

Two gunshots broke the evening calm.

Missing

MORNING BROKE and Derrick crawled from his tent feeling like he had a mouthful of cotton. The air still held the morning hush. Derrick walked to the edge of the camp and unzipped his pants to relieve himself as Jo walked from around a tree. Derrick felt his face flush.

"Well this is awkward," he tried to smile as he finished and hurriedly zipped his pants. "What are you doing out here?"

"Same thing," she smiled, "only I found someplace a little more private."

"I'll keep that in mind next time."

"Have you seen Mandy? She's not in her tent."

"Have you checked Clay's tent? Those two seemed to have gotten pretty close lately."

"Just because their close doesn't mean she's fucking him."

"Jesus, Jo, ease up a little. It was just a suggestion."

"I checked everyone's tent, she's not here," Jo informed him.

"Wait... what? When did you check everyone's tent?"

Jo stared at him for a brief second, "I got up to pee and noticed her tent was opened. She wasn't inside. I checked everywhere and I can't find her."

"Maybe she's watering the bushes too."

"I don't think so. She wouldn't wander off by herself."

"Well, she is a cop... and she's armed."

"Who's armed?" Clay asked as he walked up and stood next to Derrick.

"Mandy," Jo answered, "She... she wasn't with you last night, was she?"

"No," Clay answered as he unzipped his pants.

"Dude, there's a lady present," Derrick said quickly.

"Don't have time," Clay answered, "I'll piss my pants if I wait. She doesn't have to look."

Jo shook her head and rolled her eyes. "Men. I'm going to wake the others why you boys try to write your names in the snow."

Clay looked at Derrick puzzled, "It's not snowing."

Derrick laughed than ran to help Jo.

"You woke me up for this?" Slade said, wiping the sleep from his eyes.

"Mandy is missing," Jo repeated, "we need to find her."

"She's dead," Slade said as he climbed out of his tent and stretched the kink out of his back.

"What do you mean, she's dead?" Jo grabbed him by the collar.

"Get this crazy bitch off me!" Slade said as he struggled to free himself from her grip.

Big Jim and Derrick pulled Jo away then stepped up to Slade.

"Explain yourself," Derrick said as Slade fixed his ruffled

clothes.

"Duh... we're supposed to solve a murder, remember? Can't have a murder without a murder victim. Someone must have snuck into the camp while we were sleeping and smuggled her out."

"That actually makes sense," Big Jim answered.

"No, it doesn't," Jo argued. "Mandy wouldn't just leave without telling me."

"What are you, her mother?" Slade asked sarcastically. "Or maybe you two have some sort of lezbo thing going on?"

Clay grabbed Slade by the collar, "One of these days I'm gonna shove my fist down that smart-ass mouth of yours."

"Get your fucking hands off me Injun," Slade snapped back, his right hand unsnapping the clasp to his revolver.

Big Jim stepped between them and grabbed Slade's hand. "Enough!"

He glared at Slade, "If I ever see you reach for your gun against a fellow officer, I will report you."

Slade snorted a laugh.

"Try that shit again," Derrick said, "and I'll shoot you myself. So quit screwing around and let's get to work." He glared at Slade then turned to face the others.

"One of two things happened here last night," Derrick explained. "Either Mandy was taken as part of the Ops Training like Slade suggested, or something *has* happened to her. Either way, we are cops, so it's time we do the cop thing and figure it out."

Slade started humming the theme song to *SWAT*. Clay rolled his eyes.

"Okay," Derrick said, "this whole camp is one big crime scene so let's do this by the numbers. Jo, you and Big Jim check Mandy's tent for any signs of a struggle. Clay, you check the perimeter for anything unusual. Slade, you're with me."

"Doing what?" Slade asked.

"Staying out of *their* way. Start by checking the van to see if anything was taken."

They all nodded in agreement.

"Okay boys and girls," Derrick ordered, "we trampled over the crime scene long enough. It's time to play cops and robbers and find some clues as to what in the hell really happened last night."

Gun drawn, Slade advanced towards their van as Jo and Big Jim headed towards Mandy's tent. Derrick watched Clay circle the camp, head down, studying the ground as he walked. At one point, Clay crouched down and examined a small bush. He motioned for Derrick to join him.

"Broken twigs," Clay explained as he stood up and pointed. "Looks like someone went through here, and there's more signs over there heading down to the clearing."

"Two people?" Derrick asked.

"Maybe," Clay answered as the rest of the squad joined them. "It's hard to say without actually following the trail for a bit. It could be two, or it could be just one person backtracking to throw us off the trail."

"I thought you Indians were supposed to be good at this tracking shit? You don't even know if it's more than one person!" Slade rolled his eyes. "You're not much help, are you?"

"I said it was hard to say without actually following the trail," Clay answered, staring at Slade. "Maybe if you cleaned the shit out of your ears you'd learn something."

Slade glared at him, his top lip quivering into a hint of a snarl.

"The tent is clean," Jo announced to break the tension, "No sign of a struggle. What about the van, Slade?"

"Van's clear," Slade answered in a monotone voice, "but the distributor is gone. We're not driving out of here."

"I'm going to head down into the clearing and check out that hunting blind," Clay said as he double-checked the rounds in his firearm.

"I'm going with you," Jo said as she pushed her way past Slade. "I want to help find Mandy."

"Just stay behind me," Clay cautioned her.

Jo placed her hands on her hips defiantly, "I can take care of myself."

"I'm sure you can," Clay said as he placed a comforting hand on her shoulder, "but I can't find their tracks if you're trampling all over them. So stay behind me."

Jo smiled. "Whatever you say, Chief."

Clay smiled; Slade rolled his eyes. "Fuckin' typical."

Everyone looked at Slade, bewildered.

"I call him Chief and I'm an asshole, but if a set of tits says it, then it's okay?"

Derrick placed a hand on Slade's shoulder, "That's because you *are* an asshole."

Everyone chuckled as Slade shrugged free. The tension had subsided for a moment, but a few seconds of silence allowed the tension to creep back in.

Clay nodded to Jo then led the way down the small hill towards the clearing. Seconds later, the rest of the group turned towards the camp.

"So what's for breakfast?" Slade said as he kicked the dead embers of the campfire.

"Breakfast?" Derrick said with distaste. "We need to find Mandy."

"For Christ's sake," Slade said, "this is all just a game. A few of the boys from the academy snuck her out as part of the training op. We can't fight crime on empty stomachs so let's get a fire going and eat."

"I am kinda hungry," Big Jim said absentmindedly.

"Whatever," Derrick said as his eyes followed Big Jim's gaze. "I'm going to head down the road a bit and see if there are any tire tracks. I doubt that whoever is behind this walked all the way up here on foot."

Derrick looked at Big Jim and tried to follow his line of sight again. "What's on your mind, big guy?"

"Has anyone checked that old house?"

Derrick looked at Slade who shrugged his shoulders.

"Maybe Mandy went exploring in there and, I dunno, the floor gave out and she got knocked unconscious or something."

"Not a bad idea," Derrick said as he patted Big Jim on the shoulder. "Let's go check it out."

"Fuckin' brilliant," Slade laughed as he busied himself

building a campfire.

"What is your problem?' Derrick turned to face Slade.

"Me? I don't have a problem. You on the other hand…"

"What?"

"So what you're telling me is you guys think the tiniest member of our rag-tag little group here went exploring in a house that's as old as these hills and fell through the floor."

"What's your point?" Derrick asked impatiently.

"So your brilliant plan is that the two biggest guys are going to go in after her? If the floor couldn't support her… well, you do the math."

"You know," Derrick said with a half-grin, "for once, he's right." Slade smiled and bowed regally. Derrick's smiled broadened, "And that's why *you* should check it out."

Slade lost his smile. "Me? I'm making breakfast."

"Big Jim used to work as a short-order cook. He can take care of breakfast while we check out the house."

Slade glared at Derrick.

"And by *we*," Derrick added, "I mean *I* am heading down the road to look for tire tracks and *you* are going inside the house."

Slade looked from Derrick to the old house and back again.

"Whatever man, just hurry the fuck up cuz I'm starving."

Officer Down, Part 1

CLAY AND Jo reached the bottom of the hill; Clay motioned for her to crouch down low.

"There's a heel print here," Clay whispered as he pointed to the grassy field. "The ground is pretty solid but it's a deep impression. That means the person who made it is either very heavy…"

"Or carrying something," Jo whispered in response. "Or someone."

Clay nodded his agreement. His eyes followed a trail hidden to all but the trained eye. His gaze followed an invisible line towards the solitary apple tree that stood proudly in the middle of the clearing. He could see the fallen apples that were crushed by human boots. The nearly undetectable trail continued its crossing to the opposite side of the clearing where the hunting blind sat silently waiting.

With a shake of his hand, Clay signaled they should circle around the clearing and stay hidden in the safety of the trees.

"I'll go this way," Jo whispered. "You go that way and we'll meet at the blind."

Clay shook his head and whispered, "We should stick together."

"If they see us coming," Jo argued, "We're screwed. If we split up, we can box them in."

Clay stared at her for a long moment, then reluctantly nodded in agreement. Jo winked then silently disappeared into the brush.

Clay unholstered his pistol then set out in the opposite direction. Ten minutes later he spotted Jo crouched behind a large, fallen tree less than thirty feet from the blind. He signaled for her to hold her position as he inched forward.

As Clay approached the hunting blind, he spotted a piece of cloth lying a few feet from the blind. He didn't have to feel the texture of the liquid covering the cloth or run any field tests to know the liquid was blood.

Gun at the ready, he took a step towards the blind, then heard a distinctive yet familiar metallic click.

The first time Clay heard that sound he was only eleven years old. A large brown bear had wandered into their reservation and attacked a thirteen-year-old girl. The doctors and the newspapers claimed the girl was lucky to have survived the attack, but Clay knew the girl did not feel lucky. The bear had mauled her angelic face, leaving her with crimson scars and a dead eye.

Clay and his father set a series of massive bear traps, their steel teeth waiting patiently, hungry for the taste of blood. Perched high in a tree, Clay silently watched the massive bear approach. He watched the trap's steel jaws slice into the bear's thick, muscled leg. Clay emptied his rifle into the massive bear, reloaded, then emptied the magazine again.

When Clay returned to the Reservation, he laid the bear's head on the girl's doorstep. Half a dozen years later he married the maimed girl and she gave him two beautiful daughters.

The familiar-sounding 'click' of the bear trap being tripped raced through Clay's memory as a blood-curdling yell escaped his throat..

Birds scattered from the safety of their nesting trees in a rush of panic.

A silent silhouette eclipsed the early morning sun and stood over Clay as he writhed in pain.

His eyes bulged in shock and recognition seconds before a knife sliced deep into his open mouth to catch his final scream.

Officer Down, Part 2

BIG JIM stood up straight still holding the frying pan of sizzling bacon. He stepped towards the edge of the hill, his eyes scanning the clearing below. His senses heightened by the scream, he listened intently as he continued to scan the clearing. Minutes later, the frying pan bounced off the ground, bacon and grease splattering on the grass as Big Jim ran down the hill. Big Jim slammed through the brush like the giant T-Rex crashing through the trees in the Jurassic Park movies.

On the opposite side of the clearing, Jo raced towards him. Big Jim slowed just as Jo fell forward; he caught her in his massive arms. He pulled her behind the solitary tree in the middle of the field as he stared at the ominous-looking hunting blind, then scanned the tree line.

The morning calm had returned; Birds returned to their singing as Jo buried her face into Big Jim's chest, softly sobbing.

Several long minutes later, Derrick appeared at the top of the hill, then quickly made his way down to the clearing and raced towards them. He dropped to one knee next to Big Jim, gun drawn, his eyes scanning the surroundings as Jo sobbed an almost incoherent story about bear traps and Clay being dead.

"Stay with her!" Derrick ordered as he snapped his gun's safety to off.

"Wait," Big Jim started to argue.

"Stay with her," Derrick repeated as he darted across the clearing to the safety of the trees. Reaching over his head he grabbed a tree branch and snapped it free. With his gun at the ready, Derrick poked the stick at the ground and slowly made his way towards the blind.

When he reached Clay's body, rage helped him fight the urge to vomit. Pressing forward, he continued to check for additional traps with the tree branch until he reached the door of the hunting blind. He took a few deep breaths to calm his nerves.

As he slowly reached his hand forward to unlatch the rickety old door, a twig snapped behind him.

Derrick's breath caught in his throat as he spun around, his trigger finger moving off the side of the gun towards the trigger just as recognition grabbed hold.

"Jesus Slade, I almost shot you!" Derrick said as he relaxed his grip and lowered his weapon away from Slade.

"Where the hell did you come from?" Derrick asked.

"I heard screaming," Slade answered. "I saw Big Jim run down the hill towards Jo. I made my way along the tree line on the other side."

Derrick looked back towards the solitary apple tree in the middle of the clearing. Big Jim was still crouched down scanning the tree line with his gun drawn; a protective arm still around Jo.

Derrick turned to face Slade and nodded towards the door. He raised three fingers, then two, then one. He pushed the door but it didn't move. A second later he threw his shoulder into the door; it flew open with a loud crack.

Derrick raced in, checking straight ahead then to the left. Slade followed, aiming his gun directly ahead, then to the right to finish clearing the blind. Each remained motionless as they waited for their eyes to finish adjusting to the gloomy light. The seconds slowly dragged by before they finally lowered their weapons.

"Whoever killed Clay," Derrick said as he clicked his safety to the on position, "didn't come from this blind."

"What makes you say that?" Slade asked. "Wait… Clay is dead? What the fuck happened?""

"Yes," Derrick answered, "he's dead. He got caught in a bear trap, then was stabbed in the face."

Slade silently mouthed, "Fuck!"

"As for the blind," Derrick explained, "the door was stuck. There's no way the killer could have come out of this blind without alerting him."

"Jesus… that means…"

"That means," Derrick continued, "we have a psycho on our hands who not only likes to be up close and personal for the kill, but they're ballsy enough to walk up to an armed cop to do it."

Slade whistled softly.

"Come on," Derrick said, "let's get back to the others and find out what Jo knows."

Coming Unglued

"I DIDN'T see anything," Jo explained as Big Jim attended to the small cut on the back of her head. "We were making our way towards the blind from opposite sides of the tree line. Next thing I knew, I was face down in the dirt trying to collect my bearings. I must have only been out for a minute. When I realized what had happened, I rushed over to where Clay was and that's when I…" She sighed remorsefully. "That's when I found him."

"I heard a scream," Big Jim explained, "but I didn't see anything for several minutes. Nothing was moving, but then I saw Jo running from the tree line so I ran down to meet her."

"I heard the scream too," Derrick explained, "so I came back here. Slade came behind me and we checked out the blind. It was empty. It looks like it hasn't been used for quite some time."

"Slade came behind you?" Jo asked. "How is that possible?"

Derrick looked at her, "What do you mean?"

Slade repeated the question, "Yeah, what do you mean?"

"If you were down the road looking for tracks," Jo explained, "and Slade was in the old house at the top of the hill, how did you reach the blind first? He should have been down there ahead of you, not behind you."

Everyone looked at Slade. Slade's gun hand twitched nervously.

"Just wait a fuckin' minute," Slade said, looking from face to face, "I ran down behind Big Jim! When he cut across the field, I flanked it to the right inside the tree line and took the long way around. That's when I met up with Derrick."

Jo pulled her weapon and aimed it at Slade.

"What reason would you have for going into the tree line other than to avoid being seen?"

"Because I didn't know who the hell was screaming or why," Slade snapped back. "You'd have to be an idiot to run down the middle of an open field when there's a possible killer on the loose."

Slade looked at Big Jim, "No offence big guy, but it was kinda dumb."

"I was more concerned about Jo." Big Jim answered.

"And, for the record," Slade explained, "if I *was* the killer, which I'm not, why would I go through the hassle of tramping through the thick brush inside the tree line? It's not like I would be in any danger *if* I was the killer... so obviously, I'm not."

"I'm not buying it." Jo didn't lower her weapon. "I didn't say anything before because there wasn't enough evidence to press charges, but I heard through the grapevine a very interesting story about you, Slade. I didn't believe it... until now."

"What the hell are you talking about?" Slade asked.

"Someone damned near beat a man to death in Halifax," Jo answered. "And *you* were the primary suspect."

"Now wait just a goddamned minute!"

"And," Jo added, "the victim was an indigenous man. We've

all heard your racist remarks about Clay. That proves---"

"That doesn't prove shit!" Slade said, cutting her off.

Derrick looked from Jo to Slade. "Is what she's saying about you true?"

Slade's reflexes kicked in and he reached for his gun. Big Jim grabbed his hand in a vice-like grip to prevent him from drawing his weapon. Slade didn't even try to resist; he just opened his palms in a gesture of being non-combative.

"Slade," Derrick asked, his gun hand started to flex near his gun holster, "what happened in Halifax?"

"I lost my temper, okay? Some low-life gangbanger was screwing my kid sister... and I went too far. But that has nothing to do with what happened here. I didn't do this! Clay and I had our disagreements, and maybe I rode him pretty hard, but god-dammit man, we're all on the same team! Some maniac is out there killing us off one by one, but it wasn't me."

Derrick studied Slade for a long minute before he raised his hand and gently guided Jo's gun towards the ground.

"He's right..."

"What?" Jo objected.

"He's right," Derrick repeated. "We're all on the same team here… until there's evidence that proves otherwise. The last thing we need right now is to start turning on each other."

"But you raced him to the blind!" Jo argued.

"It doesn't look good," Derrick said, "but it's circumstantial at best."

Jo opened her mouth to object; Derrick didn't give her the chance.

"Think about it Jo, it doesn't prove anything. Hell, you were awake this morning before any of us when Mandy went missing. Does that automatically mean that you took her?"

Jo's nostrils flared as she inhaled; she wasn't impressed with the turn of events.

"From now on," Derrick added, "no one goes anywhere alone."

"What's our next move?" Big Jim asked as he released Slade's hand.

Derrick looked around. "We go back to camp---"

"What about Clay?" Big Jim asked. "We can't just leave him here."

"We're not going to," Derrick answered. "We go back to camp, grab our field kits and start gathering evidence. Once we swab for DNA, take some photos, and clear the area, we'll move his body back to the van."

An uncomfortable silence hung in the air.

"This is beginning to feel more and more like an episode of CSI," Big Jim said more to himself than to anyone else.

"Or a Patricia Cornwell novel," Jo added.

"One thing all those crime shows and books have in common," Derrick reminded them, "the killer *always* makes a mistake. It's our job to find it."

Missing Pieces

THEY ALL gathered around the large plastic sheet they spread on the ground. They didn't have the luxury of a table, so the evidence and polaroid's they collected were organized neatly on the plastic sheet.

"Here's what we know," Derrick said as he studied the evidence. "There's no foreign DNA under Clay's fingernails, nothing to indicate a struggle, and his gun was drawn but never fired. I think when he stepped in the trap the Suspect took that opportunity to finish him off."

Big Jim exhaled sharply, "What a miserable way to go."

"Why a knife?" Slade asked as he examined the pictures.

"Best guess," Derrick said as he continued his assessment, "it's silent. Shooting a gun would alert us that something was wrong."

"Well I don't know about that," Slade argued, "he was screaming in pain. That trap damn near cut his leg clean off. Even without the coup de grâce, he probably would have bled out, or died of shock. We're cops, not doctors. Our basic first aid training probably wouldn't have helped Clay all that much. At best, we woulda just delayed the inevitable, so why risk being seen just to stab him?"

"There's a lot of unanswered questions. It was a huge risk to rely on a trap." Derrick looked down over the hill towards the blind then back to his fellow officers. "The blind was perfect cover and easy to defend. The suspect could have easily picked us off with a rifle from that position, but they decided to not use the blind and set a trap instead? Risky move considering Clay's a skilled tracker."

"Apparently not skilled enough," Slade added absentmindedly. Derrick shot him a dirty look.

"What? I'm just stating the obvious. Of all people, he's the one that should have seen it."

"I don't think it was meant for Clay," Big Jim pointed out.

"He's too smart for that. I think the trap was left there by a hunter. Clay was just in the wrong place at the wrong time."

Jo watched each man intently as they spoke but remained silent.

"Clay's too good," Slade added, "to be taken out by a trap. He had to have been focused on something else not to see it. Maybe that piece of bloodied cloth we found. I think Jim's right, the trap wasn't part of the Suspect's plan, he just took advantage of the situation to finish Clay off."

"Careful Slade," Derrick almost smiled, "you're giving Clay a compliment."

"Listen, guys," Slade announced, "I know I'm an asshole, okay? Right or wrong, I have my reasons. But this? No way. I never liked Clay, that's no big secret. Hell, I don't even like any of you clowns, but that doesn't make me the killer."

"None of us like you either," Big Jim shot back.

"Clay mentioned another set of tracks heading off in that direction," Derrick pointed to the east. "He also mentioned it could be two people, which makes sense. Either it's one very athletic person to move around so quickly, or there's more than one suspect."

"Two people staying out of sight this entire time?" Big Jim suggested. "Seems risky."

Derrick cleared his throat, "Here's what we know: He, or they, took Mandy out from under our noses without making a sound. We still don't know where she is."

"Or if she's even alive?" Slade added.

"Considering how brutally Clay was killed," Derrick explained, "it doesn't make sense that the suspect, or suspects, would go through the risk of sneaking her out of camp just to kill her. He, or they, would have just killed her while she slept. So I think she's alive, we just have to find her."

"What else do we know?" Big Jim asked.

"They didn't take any of our gear," Derrick reminded them, "but they disabled the van."

"Doesn't make sense," Slade noted. "Why leave a group of cops all their gear, and their guns, but disable the van?"

"That's the million-dollar question," Derrick answered. "Either they are extremely confident in their skills and are playing the long game... or they're extremely dumb."

"Or maybe we're just looking at this all wrong," Slade suggested.

"What do you mean?" Jo asked.

"Occam's razor," Slade suggested, "the simplest solution is often the correct one. We're going on a lot of assumptions, but we are overlooking the obvious."

"Which is what?" Derrick asked.

"We are up here on a training operation, right?"

The others nodded.

"So it makes sense, for an Op, to smuggle out one of our own so we have something to investigate, right?'

"More or less," Derrick answered.

"What if Clay stepping in that trap was an accident, pure and simple? What if he saw a poacher with a loaded weapon, which startled him and caused him to step in the trap, and then the poacher panicked? The guy is out here hunting illegally and sees a man with a police jacket and his weapon drawn just before he steps into the poacher's bear trap. Maybe the poacher just panicked and killed him to make sure he doesn't go to jail. People do strange things when they panic. Maybe we're taking two unrelated incidents, Mandy missing and Clay getting killed, and filling in pieces and drawing conclusions that aren't even there?"

"That kinda makes sense," Big Jim agreed.

"It does make sense," Derrick said as he scanned the area again, "but let me play the devil's advocate. Let's say Clay's accident is just that, an accident, and let's say someone woke Mandy up in the middle of the night and smuggled her out as part of the Op. There's just one problem... a few pieces of the puzzle are still missing."

"Like what?" Slade asked.

"Like why disable the van? If the Op is to solve a murder mystery, why strand us up here?" Derrick looked at each of his fellow officers.

"If the people organizing the Op were up here, surely they would have heard the screaming. They would at least come to investigate what is going on. Plus," Derrick continued, "the Op is supposed to be solving a mock murder. We can't have a murder without a body, so why take Mandy? Why not just give her a sign that says 'victim' and order her to play dead? We're supposed to gather evidence and solve a fake murder for the Op. There is no evidence, she just vanished without a trace."

"Or maybe we just didn't find the clues?" Big Jim suggested.

"Maybe," Derrick nodded, then added, "or maybe there's none to be found. Maybe some psycho is out there picking off cops one by one. I don't know what in the hell is going on, but I'd rather be a bit paranoid and assume the worst and live to tell about it, than assume it's all a big coincidence and be next on the killer's list."

They all nodded in agreement.

"So what do we do now?" Slade asked.

"We stick to the plan," Derrick answered.

Slade scratched his head. "Did I miss something? Do we even have a plan?"

"We do," Derrick answered. "We stick together, we find Mandy, then we get the hell off this mountain."

Slade looked at the van. "On foot?"

Derrick nodded.

"Okay, Slade, you and Big Jim head over there and try to pick up the trail Clay spotted. Jo and I will head down the road and try to find signs of another vehicle. If there is a killer on the loose, I doubt they walked up here. We have them outnumbered and outgunned, so if someone is out there set out on killing us, let's find this fucker and put a bullet in his head."

Slade pulled his revolver and smiled, "It's about fuckin' time!"

Suspect

DERRICK AND Jo walked side by side down the old mountain road in a slow but steady pace. Their heads moved side to side in rhythm to their steps. Their eyes were constantly scanning the tree lines for any sign of movement.

"This is as far as I made it last time," Derrick said without looking at Jo. "That's when I heard the scream and headed back. You said you used to camp near here when you were a kid; any place along this road to hide a vehicle?"

"Too many," Jo answered. "There are countless logging roads all over this mountain. If the suspect is on an ATV, they can pretty much go anywhere and hide anywhere they like. This is a waste of time, we should head back."

Derrick didn't reply.

"I'm worried about Slade," Jo said, stopping to take a drink from her canteen.

"I know you are," Derrick answered, "but I don't think he's our guy."

"He's been riding Clay pretty hard, then this whole thing about beating up that First Nations guy in Halifax… and… it just feels wrong."

"Slade is an asshole, I'll give you that, but a murderer? He's a prejudiced prick, there's no doubt about that, but even that doesn't make him a murderer.

"If you say so."

"Jo?" Derrick asked.

"What?"

"Where are your glasses?"

"What?" Jo look confused.

"You're glasses. I've never seen you without them before."

"Oh, I..." Jo's smiled, sheepishly, "I honestly don't know. I guess I must have lost them when I got knocked out."

"I thought you couldn't see without them."

"I can't read without them," she corrected him.

"You seemed to be doing okay when we were gathering and reviewing the evidence."

"Honestly," Jo answered, "with so much going on, I never even noticed. But that would explain this splitting headache I have."

"We'll have to go back to where you were attacked and find them."

"I wouldn't worry about it," she answered, "they're probably smashed anyway."

Derrick studied her for a few seconds then slowly nodded.

"I still don't trust Slade," Jo said as she took another drink from her canteen. "He arrived at the blind after you... and---"

"And nothing," Derrick said, cutting her off. "I know his kind. He talks a big game, but it's mostly just talk. Maybe he goes too far and doesn't know when to shut up. I wouldn't put it past him if he really did beat that guy in Halifax… but as mad as he was about his little sister, he didn't kill him. I don't think he has what it takes to kill someone in cold blood.

"Maybe you're right," Jo answered.

"I better be… or Big Jim's in a heap of trouble right now."

Big Jim & Slade

SLADE AND Big Jim reached the edge of a forgotten graveyard. The wind had risen; each gust sent haunting whispers through the grass and made the tall birch trees rattle their dying leaves. The graveyard had a gloomy and wild look to it. Brambles and tall weeds grew on the graves and clinging ivy swarmed over the crumbling granite.

Slade slowed his pace. He was a few feet behind Big Jim when he slowly drew his weapon. He stopped and raised his pistol.

Moments later, Big Jim, aware that Slade was no longer beside him, stopped and turned to look behind him. Slade aimed carefully and gently squeezed the trigger.

Big Jim's eyes opened wide as the sound of Slade's gun echoed off the tombstones. A yelp reverberated in the old graveyard as Big Jim hit the ground.

Slade took aim again as Big Jim, panicked with fear and adrenaline, struggled to release his gun from its holster.

Another shot pierced the air and a second yelp resounded in the once quiet graveyard.

Derrick and Jo froze. An instant later they were running at full speed back the way they came. Lungs burning, Derrick ran past the camp and into the woods. Jo kept pace a few yards back. When Derrick reached the graveyard he saw Big Jim sitting on the ground, holding his head between his legs and Slade, gun drawn, standing over him.

"Drop it!" Derrick yelled, his gun aimed at Slade. Slade spun towards Derrick and raised his hands.

"Wait a second---"

"Drop the fuckin' gun... NOW!" Derrick ordered as he drew nearer. Slade slowly clicked the safety on his weapon and gently laid it on the ground.

"Jim, are you okay?" Derrick asked.

Big Jim didn't answer, he just looked at Derrick, fear masked his usually calm expression.

"What the fuck?" Jo asked through heavy breaths when she finally caught up to them.

"Jim, are you hurt?" Derrick asked.

Big Jim swallowed a lump in his throat. "Just my pride. I think I shit myself."

Derrick shot a glance at Big Jim then back to Slade.

"What the hell happened?"

Big Jim wiped his brow then staggered to his feet. "Davey Crockett here spotted some coyotes and shot at them."

Derrick's brow furrowed. "What?"

"Coyotes," Slade explained, "nasty fuckin' things, vicious too. There was a small pack of them over there." Slade pointed behind Big Jim. "I got two of them, now will you get that fuckin' gun out of my face?"

Derrick lowered his weapon and snapped the safety on.

"When I saw him draw his gun," Big Jim explained, "I thought for sure I was a goner. My whole life flashed before my eyes when I heard that first shot."

Slade smiled. "Sorry big man, I didn't want to spook them."

Big Jim looked at Derrick then, without warning, threw a straight right at Slade. It connected flush. Slade's head snapped back from the impact as his legs buckled.

Big Jim looked down at Slade laying on the ground then back to Derrick, "When he wakes up, tell him that was for scaring the shit outta me."

Derrick chuckled, then bent down to help Slade.

"You're okay," Derrick said as Slade slowly regained consciousness. "You were on the losing end of Jim's rage. Can't say that I blame him."

When Slade's eyes were no longer glossy, Derrick helped him to a sitting position. A couple of minutes later, with the help of Derrick and Jo, Slade was finally able to stand.

"Next time," Slade said through a mouthful of blood, "I think I'll just spook the coyotes."

He looked at Big Jim and offered his hand.

"Sorry, Jim," Slade said solemnly.

Big Jim shook his hand then bent down, picked up Slade's gun and handed it to him.

Slade took it and holstered it.

"Let's head back," Jo said as she turned to leave.

Shallow Grave

"HOLD UP," Slade said, "that many coyotes clustered together, heads down, means they were eating something."

"It's getting late," Jo argued, "and I think we've had enough excitement for one day. We really don't need to look at some dead animal coyotes were eating.

"Then you go on ahead," Slade answered, "Because I do want to see."

No one moved.

"It could be Mandy," Slade added.

The three men looked back and forth at each other, silently confirming that they did have to go check. They walked towards the spot where Slade saw the coyotes. Jo sighed and reluctantly followed.

"Is that?" Slade started to say.

"Oh shit, no!!" Big Jim yelled as he raced ahead of the others. He fell to his knees and started clawing at the ground. A hand with painted fingernails was protruding from a small mound of dirt. Two of its fingers were missing, eaten by a hungry coyote while its companions dug at the ground to unbury the corpse.

"Mandy!" Big Jim yelled as he scratched at the dirt. "Jesus... no!"

Slade and Derrick fell to their knees at his side and started scraping at the ground to help. Jo dropped down beside them and pushed handfuls of dirt out of the way.

They brushed the last of the dirt off the blood-soaked carpet and in unison, they stopped. Each fought to catch their breath... and their nerve.

Derrick exhaled deeply. His pulse raced through his body. His shaking hands reached forward and slowly pulled the carpet back to reveal the victim's face.

Long, torturous seconds passed as they stared at the woman buried in the shallow grave.

Big Jim finally broke the deafening silence. "Who the hell is that?"

"Well... it ain't Mandy," Slade said in a soft voice.

Derrick stared at the corpse. Like the name of an old acquaintance he had not seen in years, recognition sat on the edge of his tongue but refused to be identified. He knew the name, but it just wouldn't come out. His mouth moved slightly in a pattern that resembled speech, but sound did not cross his lips. His mind was thoroughly busy trying to solve the mystery; too busy to speak actual words.

"Fuck me," Slade said at last. "Isn't that the chick from the store?"

"Who?" Big Jim asked, his gaze shifting from the corpse to Slade, then back again.

"The hot cop I was flirting with when we picked up the van in Montague."

Recognition slammed home.

"It is," Derrick confirmed. "Officer Roberts."

"Jesus," Big Jim said as he looked around. "How'd she get way out here?"

"More importantly," Derrick said as he un-holstered his gun, "where the hell is her partner?"

Camp

THE SHADOWS were getting longer as the sun began to dip below the mountains, casting an ominous, orangish-red light across the entire camp.

Derrick and Slade moved Clay's body from the van to one of the tents while Big Jim and Jo lined the hard, metal floor of the van with sleeping bags, though no one expected to get any sleep that night.

As darkness enveloped the camp, a bitter wind shook the trees and surrounding brush. The constant sound of owls, crickets and frogs, combined with creaking trees and animals scurrying around the forest floor, created a cacophony of uneasiness. Despite their apprehensions, exhaustion from the day's events grabbed hold and they drifted off to sleep.

A cold breeze from the van's open door woke Derrick. Gun in hand, he slowly moved to the door and spotted Jo, who was bent down with one of the sleeping bags wrapped around her.

"What are you doing?" Derrick asked, startling her.

"What?" She looked at him for a long moment. "Tying my shoe."

"No, I mean what are you doing outside?" Derrick stared at her, trying to read her expression in the dim light before the moon hid behind the clouds.

"Oh… I gotta pee."

"Now?"

"Can't hold it any longer."

"I don't think that's a good idea."

"I don't think it's a good idea to freeze my ass off squatting in the woods either… but here we are… and I still can't hold it any longer."

"Okay," Derrick said as he climbed out of the van. "I'll go with you."

"Excuse me?" Jo said as she placed her hands on her hips.

"Just to stand guard," Derrick explained. "I don't want you getting caught with your pants down."

Jo stared at him. "That's not funny."

"It wasn't meant to be," Derrick replied as he grabbed a sleeping bag to protect himself against the cold night air.

A few feet into the woods, Jo shivered as she squatted next to a large oak tree.

"This is embarrassing," Jo said as she stared at Derrick's back. "I can't go with you standing there."

Derrick chuckled. "Would it help if I whipped it out and peed too?"

"That's quite alright," Jo laughed. "I seen it once already this weekend. You can keep *that* weapon in your pants."

Derrick laughed quietly. A few moments later she patted him on the shoulder that she was finished. They walked back to the camp in silence.

"Where's Slade?' Jo asked when she opened the van door.

Derrick looked around then shook Big Jim awake.

"Jim, have you seen Slade? Did you hear anything?"

"Huh? What? I... I didn't hear anything," Big Jim answered as he wiped the sleep from his eyes.

"Shit," Derrick said as he unholstered his weapon, "we gotta go find him."

"Derrick," Jo interrupted, "we're not going to find him in the dark with a couple of Maglites. We're gonna have to wait until morning."

"By morning he could be dead."

"By morning," Jo argued, "we all could be dead if we go out there. We have the home team advantage by staying in the van. Out there the killer has the advantage."

"He's just as blind as we are," Derrick tried to explain.

"Unless he has night vision goggles," Big Jim suggested, "then he holds all the cards. Jo's right, we're sitting ducks out there."

"We don't know if he has night vision," Derrick argued.

"We don't know he doesn't," Jo answered. "Besides, you're the one who told us that Clay said there might be two of them. Hell, even you said there might be two of them. Now you want us to go out there with nothing but a couple of flashlights and no idea where to even start looking?"

Jo placed her hand on Derrick's shoulder. "We both know you took it upon yourself to be responsible for the team... but Derrick," Jo said as she gently brushed the side of his face, "We are not your responsibility Sweetie. I'm sorry, but when push comes to shove, I value my own life more than that self-righteous, arrogant shit-head. I'm not getting myself killed stumbling around in a dark forest looking for someone like Slade when he's probably already dead."

Derrick placed his hand over Jo's, looked deep into her eyes, then pulled her hand away.

"That's the difference between you and me," Derrick said as he double-checked the magazine in his Beretta, "I care about other people. Even self-righteous, arrogant shit-heads like Slade. Stay here if you want, but I'm not going to sit around while a member of my team is in trouble."

Derrick flicked his Maglite on then started searching the ground for clues. Big Jim stepped out of the van and placed a comforting hand on Jo's shoulder.

"It's okay to be scared. There's no love lost between me and Slade, but Derrick is right. We have to stick together."

Jo rolled her eyes. "Whatever. Let's just go find him so we can go back to bed. The dumb shit probably went to take a dump and got lost in the woods."

Derrick shone his light at Jo and Big Jim and clicked it on and off a few times. A minute later they were standing by his side.

"Look," Derrick said shining his light on a broken branch, "I think they went through here."

Derrick followed the path with Jo behind him and Big Jim bringing up the rear.

"Should we yell his name or something, just in case the dumb shit is lost?" Big Jim asked.

"Can't risk giving away our position," Derrick answered.

"I think our flashlights took care of that," Jo answered. "We need to split up. We're never going to find him if we're all looking at the same damn trees."

"Bad idea," Derrick said as he turned to face them, "we need to stick together."

"We need to go back to the van," Jo argued, "but since you're the one who insisted that we look for him, let's quit fuckin' around like a couple of amateurs and spread out. We'll cover three times as much ground."

Big Jim shrugged his shoulders.

"Fine," Derrick reluctantly agreed, "lets spread out. But try to keep each other in sight. Jo, you stay in the middle."

Jo snorted a laugh. "Always the protector. Let's just get this over with, and so help me, if I find out we're out here freezing our asses off all because that dumb shit just got lost, I'll shoot him myself."

Jo and Big Jim headed west. When Jo was at the edge of Derricks sightline she stopped as Big Jim continued walking. Once he was in position, they all started working their way forward.

Derrick walked around a cluster of spruce trees. When he emerged again, Jo's silhouette in the moonlight, and the light of her Maglite, had disappeared.

"Jo," Derrick whispered loudly, "Jo. Goddammit, where are you?" He shone his Maglite, but the windblown trees made it impossible to detect movement. Everything was swaying in the wind.

Derrick cautiously made his way towards her last known position when two gunshots echoed in the trees, the muzzle flashes briefly lit up the forest.

The quick flashes of light, and the crack of a Beretta, chased Derrick's caution away. He raced through the forest. Branches slapped at his face and arms; it didn't slow his pace. He pressed forward, desperately searching the forest floor for his worst nightmare... another fallen comrade.

Moments later, his nightmare laid at his feet.

Big Jim was on his back. glassy eyes stared helplessly at the night sky. Derrick dropped to his knees trying to stop the bleeding. Blood poured from Big Jim's neck with every laboured breath; his blood-soaked chest left no question as to whether or not the second bullet found its mark.

Big Jim's frightened eyes begged Derrick to understand, to see what he saw, but his gurgled voice could not form audible words.

"Shhh, you're going to be okay," Derrick lied. "Just relax buddy, and don't try to talk."

Big Jim's massive hand grabbed Derrick by the arm and squeezed. A sudden onslaught of coughing flushed more blood from his system.

Derrick took Big Jim's hand and squeezed; nothing. He watched the light from Big Jim's unblinking eyes fade with a final, guttural cough. Derrick blinked slowly, then reached over and closed Big Jim's eyes for the final time.

"Arrrrghhhhh!" Derrick screamed to the trees; to anyone who dared to listen, then stood up. "I'm gonna kill you mother-fucker! Come on! I'm right here! Come get me!"

The forest remained mute. Derrick dropped to his knees, buried his face in his hands, and cried.

Revelation

TEN LONG minutes later, Derrick stood and started the long, lonely walk back to the camp. Thoughts floated in and out of his mind like clouds drifting on a gentle breeze. Some thoughts stayed longer than others, but each drifted away as a new thought, a new recollection, took place.

One thought, something he had pushed to the back of his mind, had resurfaced once again. Now, this strange, foreign thought held more weight. It was more believable than before.

When he first questioned that thought, his gut instinct laid out the facts, but his heart pushed it away. It couldn't be true; it couldn't be possible. Stress and an over-active imagination, combined with guilt for even thinking it, were the weapons he used to bury that thought to the deepest recesses of his soul.

But now, as visions of his friend, the gentle giant, bleeding out on the forest floor, added more weight to the thought; making it more powerful and unyielding.

Derrick fought to squash the absurdity of it, but the damn thought would not be tamed again. Not this time. It tormented him with every step; the missing puzzle piece was now in play. His gut told him it was true, and that sinking feeling in his stomach, in his heart, refused to be pushed aside... again.

When Derrick broke free of the tree line he saw Jo crouched by the van, her head buried in her hands.

"Jo," Derrick said flatly, "Jim is dead."

Jo stood up and raced towards him. When she was less than five feet from him Derrick pointed his gun at her. She froze.

"Derrick, what are you doing?"

"You fucked up," Derrick answered calmly. Jo's expression instantly changed.

"What are you talking about? I heard the gunshots and," her tears flowed easily, "I'm sorry. I got scared and I ran."

"Killers always make a mistake," Derrick's voice was cold, unemotional. "I was just too blind to see yours."

"You're not making any sense." Jo fidgeted nervously.

"There was always something about your glasses that seemed off, but I couldn't quite put my finger on it. Until now"

"My glasses? Derrick, I think you're in shock. Maybe you should sit down."

Derrick raised his gun to point it directly at her head.

"No refraction."

"What?"

"Glasses distort the features of the person wearing them. Some just a little, others a lot. It depends on how strong the prescription is."

Jo stared at him. "You're not making any sense."

"But not yours. Your features weren't distorted when you wore them."

"So what? I wore fake glasses. Big deal. I wore them and dyed my hair to make me look smarter, so the instructors wouldn't think I'm a dumb blonde. It doesn't mean anything."

"At first I couldn't figure out why you weren't in any hurry to find your glasses when you said you lost them."

"Is there a point to all this?" Jo said impatiently.

"But then you claimed they were for reading only. Why do you need fake glasses for reading, and how can glasses you don't need give you headaches?"

Jo said nothing, she just stared at him.

"When Mandy went missing, you were up before anyone. With Clay, you claimed you were knocked out, but somehow managed to wake up, find his body, and then run half-way across the clearing before Jim made it down the hill. Then Slade goes missing and once again, your outside by yourself while everyone else is asleep."

"You need to calm down and think about what you're doing." JO said nervously.

"And let's not forget," Derrick added, "How adamant you were about not seeing what the coyotes were eating. That's because you already knew. That's why you tried to talk us into leaving."

The evil lurking behind Jo's eyes revealed itself as her expression transformed into a feral grin. It caught him off-guard. It was only a split-second, but that was all she needed to draw her weapon.

They each stood motionless as death waited patiently for one of them to pull the trigger.

"Where's Slade?" Derrick was sure he already knew the answer.

"Dead."

"How did you get him without waking anyone?"

"Easy," Jo smiled. "I just whispered sweet nothings in his ear and asked him to come with me to have sex. And, like the dog that he is, he followed. I sliced his throat while he was preoccupied unzipping his pants. Men like him are so pathetically predictable."

"Why?" was the only question Derrick had left.

"Did I ever tell you my father was a cop? Or how daddy had his own way of delivering punishment?" A tiny tear, a real tear, escaped her cold eyes as she circled Derrick. "He always told me I was special, that I was his secret princess. That the vile things he did to me were because he loved me more than my sister. Oh, I tried to fight him off, I tried to tell, but my mother was either too drunk or too scared to do anything about it. She pretended like nothing ever happened. He told me that as long as I let him do those things to me, he wouldn't need my sister to do them. For years I let that animal have his way with me to protect her, but when I finally couldn't take it anymore, I tried to make him stop."

Jo's gun hand shook as she recalled the terror. "I even called the cops, for all the good that did. What was the word of a troubled teen against a decorated officer? Of course, my mother was of no help, so eventually, I tried running away. But every goddamn time I tried to escape the stupid cops always brought me back home... to him. And what was my reward for finally standing up for myself? Thrown in a mental hospital."

Derrick matched her steps as they continued to walk in a circle, as if they were performing some type of ritual dance. Each staring the other down, each pointing a loaded weapon at the other, each ready to squeeze the trigger to end the dance.

Jo continued her story. "You would think that being locked up in a nut house would be better than living at home with that animal, but I wasn't so lucky. The orderlies took turns having their way with me, sometimes two or three at a time. No one's going to believe a crazy person, right?"

Derrick didn't answer. It was a rhetorical question.

"Well, my sister believed me. My sister knew. She was Daddy's special little angel too. She tried to get me out of that place, but it was hopeless. As long as Daddy had the cops in his pocket, I wasn't going anywhere." Jo's voice deepened; anger was grabbing hold.

"Then one day, my sister tells me she got accepted to the police academy. Can you fuckin' believe it? She wants to be a cop! I never felt so betrayed in all my life."

Jo unconsciously lowered her weapon. It wasn't much, but it was all he had. Derrick quickly stepped forward and slammed the butt of his gun into her forehead. Jo stumbled back. She tried to shoot but Derrick was too fast, too skilled, and he easily disarmed her.

"Well now, ain't you the clever one?" Jo's feral grin returned. "So what are you gonna do now, oh illustrious leader? Arrest me? We both know I won't do time. I'm crazy, remember? They'll just put me back in the institution. Then, when I break out, I'll be coming for you."

"Then I'll just shoot you and be done with it."

"Oh please, Sweety," Jo smiled, "we both know you're not gonna pull the trigger. You live for this cop shit. You're not going to throw your whole life away, ruin your career before it even gets started by shooting someone in cold blood."

Derrick did not reply. He couldn't. He knew she was right.

"For what it's worth Sweety, I never planned on hurting you."

This time Derrick found his voice, "Go fuck yourself."

Jo's laugh resonated in the surrounding trees. "Here's how this is going to play out," Jo informed him, "You are going to let me go, and then you are going to spend the rest of your life trying to track me down."

This time Derrick laughed. "What makes you think I'm going to let you go?"

"Because even if you know you can't save someone Sweety, you have to try anyway."

Derrick's brow furrowed

Jo smiled. "So who are you taking back alive? Me... or Mandy?"

"You're lying."

"Am I? Are you willing to take that chance?"

Jo stared at Derrick, her poker face gave away nothing.

"Are you willing to let poor, innocent Mandy die, just so you can arrest me?"

"You killed everyone else," Derrick blurted, "why should I believe that she's alive?"

"I'm not the only one with a troubled past. It's like a sixth sense, we can spot each other a mile away... sisters of the used and abused childhood."

"I don't believe you."

"Of course you do... you just don't know it yet." Jo's feral smile made a return visit.

"Poor, sweet and innocent Mandy dealt with her past by partying it up. I tried to teach her to have more respect for herself, but she was a partier, that's for sure. That's why I decided to give her a little wakeup call that night on campus"

"She said she fell down some stairs."

Jo laughed boisterously, "Oh please… you're too smart not to know that story was a pile of horse shit."

"Where is she?"

"As long as you have that gun trained on me, you'll never know."

"And I'm supposed to believe she's alive and that you'll tell me?"

"You have to believe me, Sweety. It's in your nature. You can't go through life not knowing if there was more you could have done. It will eat you alive."

Derrick swallowed a lump.

"Don't blame yourself Sweety, it's not your fault. It's just the way you're wired: To serve and protect. So while you were trying to save Jim, I was stuffing Mandy in a trunk." Jo glanced at her watch, "I don't think she's gonna last much longer without some fresh air."

Derrick stepped towards her, "Where is she?"

"Now now," Jo said, taking a few steps back. "All you have to do is let her out and Mandy will live. If you shoot me, she dies. So lower your gun and let's talk deal."

Derrick hesitated, then slowly lowered his gun towards the ground. Jo was disarmed; if she tried anything, he knew he could raise his gun and shoot her before she took two steps. He needed her to think she had the upper hand. Part of his brain screamed that she did have the advantage, but he squashed that thought and focused his attention on Jo.

"That's better," Jo smiled. "Please don't bore me with tales of how you are going to hunt me down. We both know that's exactly what you are going to do, so let's fast forward to the good stuff, shall we?"

"What do you want?"

"To go free of course. You get to save the girl and I get to walk. It's a win-win situation if you ask me."

"I'm listening."

Jo looked at her watch again, "My how time flies. You can rush in to save her or we can stand here debating your conscience. She doesn't have much time."

"Where is she?" Derrick repeated as Jo took several more steps backwards. She was almost to the edge of the van. Derrick knew that if she reached the back of the van she could duck out of sight and disappear in the woods. He raised his weapon again.

"Where is she? Or so help me God I will---"

"I know you won't shoot, so stop pretending."

When Jo was standing at the back of the van she answered, "She's in the old house."

"You're lying!" Derrick took a step towards Jo. "Slade already checked the house."

"Did he? Really? And how well do you think that lazy, arrogant prick actually searched the entire house when he's the one who said Mandy was taken as part of the Training Op?"

Derrick hesitated.

"Bye Sweety," Jo said as she blew him a kiss and disappeared behind the van and into the woods.

"Shit," Derrick took a few steps to chase after her then stopped. He looked over his shoulder at the dilapidated old house. An instant later he was rushing towards it.

This Old House

DERRICK STEPPED inside and was immediately greeted with the unpleasant odour of mould and mildew; the chalky scent of damp plaster invaded his nostrils as he clicked on his Maglite. He worked his way to the top floor and found a large trunk sitting in the corner of what was once the master bedroom.

To the untrained eye, it just looked like an old trunk, but to Derrick, it looked like a miniature coffin held shut with a shiny, new padlock.

He raced forward. He pointed his gun at the lock then thought better of it, not wanting the bullet to pierce the old trunk, hitting Mandy.

Blood racing through his veins, he sat on the floor, braced the trunk with his feet and grabbed the padlock with both hands. He pulled until his muscles were taut with pain.

He cursed under his breath, pleaded silently with the empty room, and continued to pull.

The silence of the tomblike place was broken with the snap of breaking wood. Derrick fell back as the trunk finally let go of its lock.

He scrambled to the trunk, yanked the top open and uttered a solitary word: "Mandy."

Still groggy from the effects of the chloroform, Mandy leaned heavily on Derrick as he led her out of the house and down the old dirt road. Tall spruce and birch trees flanked them on either side. They were walking for nearly an hour when they spotted a police van stopped in the middle of the road. Derrick felt Mandy's grip tighten on him.

"Wait here," Derrick suggested as he helped Mandy sit on a large boulder off to the side of the road, "I'm going to check it out."

"Don't leave me!" Mandy begged as she grabbed his arm in a

viselike grip.

"I'll just be a minute. You'll be able to see me the whole time."

"No Derrick, please!" Her tears flowed freely, "I...."

Mandy looked at the surrounding forest. "She could be out there... watching... waiting."

"Okay," Derrick said as he helped her back to her feet. "It's okay, you're safe with me now and I'm not going to let you go."

He offered his left hand. She took it. With his right hand he clicked his Beretta's safety to the off position.

They inched forward cautiously. Derrick noticed a pool of blood on the driver's side that lead into the woods. All the tires were flat, wrapped in barbed wire that once belonged to the rotted fenceposts that lined that section of the road.

He walked Mandy over to the passenger side. He quickly glanced inside the front of the van. Empty. He aimed his weapon at the sliding side door and motioned for Mandy to pull it open. Her shaking hands gripped the handle hesitantly, then with a deep breath, pulled.

The van was empty; the radio shattered.

The blood trail leading into the woods, and the distinct smell of lingering chloroform in the van allowed Derrick to draw a mental image of what happened.

When the van got hung up on the barbed wire, Jo used chloroform to put the passenger to sleep when the driver got out to inspect the damage.

His mind drifted back to the graveyard where they found Officer Roberts, and then to a memory of the two cops waiting in front of the convenience store in Montague. The male cop was a big burly man. Too big for Jo to carry, so she most likely shot him.

It was painfully obvious that Jo had no love for cops, especially male cops, but why carry Roberts all the way to the graveyard just to kill and bury her?

Two thoughts occurred to Derrick: Either Jo was setting up some sort of elaborate plan, or something changed, and she had no choice but to kill Roberts.

"Doesn't make sense," Derrick thought out loud. "Why go through all the trouble to carry her to that gravesite just to kill her?"

"What gravesite?" Mandy asked.

"Remember the two cops from Montague that gave us the van?"

She nodded.

"We found officer Roberts buried in a shallow grave."

"Was she wrapped in a carpet?"

Derrick looked at her quizzically, "How did you know that?"

"There's a section of carpet missing from the back of that van."

Derrick nodded as Mandy batted her eyelashes, "I'm not just a pretty face you know?"

Derrick chuckled, "I know, you beat my score on the P.S.T."

"So what do you think happened?" Mandy asked.

"I don't think she meant to kill her. She doesn't like cops in general, but it's male cops she has an issue with."

"Do I need to ask why?"

Derrick remembered Jo saying they were sisters of the used and abused childhood.

"It's a long story," he said, avoiding the subject. "The point is, I think she just meant to hide her for some reason or another. Judging by the way she was killed; I'm thinking Roberts somehow managed to break free and saw Jo… that meant Jo had no choice but to kill her."

"Leaving her tied up in the woods is not exactly the best way to keep her alive," Mandy said. "Bears, coyotes, you name it… eventually, the animals would have ripped her to shreds."

"I think she planned on killing her," Derrick explained, "she could have tied her up anywhere near here and we would never have known. So why carry her all the way back to put her close to our camp?"

"Training Op," Mandy suggested.

"What do you mean?"

"Like you said," Mandy explained, "we would never have known, and she wanted us to know. If these two didn't show up for the mock murder, we all would have known something was up. And the last thing that psycho bitch wanted was for us to leave. I think she decided to use Roberts as the murder victim for her own Training Op."

"That kinda makes sense," Derrick acknowledged, "but we would have known it wasn't a fake murder as soon as we found her."

"True," Mandy agreed, "and while we were busy looking for the killer, she would be able to pick us off one by one."

"In the end," Derrick said softly, "Roberts' death was already a sure thing."

Derrick pointed at the blood trail leading into the woods.

"I don't think we have to walk very far," Derrick told her, "before we find what's left of her partner."

"There are two shell casings on the ground," Derrick pointed out, "so I'm guessing he died quickly. She probably left him where he fell, and the animals dragged him off, or he was badly wounded and dragged himself into the woods trying to escape."

"Should we go look for him? Just in case... you know, he's still alive."

Derrick looked at the pool of blood by the van and the trail of blood leading into the woods. He knew with that much blood loss there was no way that man was still alive. He also knew what Jo had said about him was true… he had to be sure; not knowing would eat him alive.

"Okay, let's go. Just remember… when we find him, it's not going to be pretty."

Not Pretty

FIVE MINUTES later, Mandy was wiping the vomit from the corners of her mouth.

Derrick's description of it not being pretty was an understatement. The animals had torn the man to shreds. What little meat he had left on his bones was covered in blood-soaked, tattered clothing.

Derrick wrapped what was left of him in a sheet of plastic from the van and Mandy helped him carry the body back. It would be a closed casket funeral, but at least his family would have a body to bury.

As they walked, Mandy occupied her mind by trying to calculate the time it took to drive to the campsite, then converted that into how long it would take to get back down the mountain on foot. Mentally it was a boring exercise, but it was the only thing that kept her other thought at bay… *Why did Jo kill the others but allowed her to live?*

Epilogue

DERRICK STONE sat in front of a large oak desk; the Chief of Police sat across from him holding Derrick's thick report.

"I read your mini-novel," the Chief told him, "now tell me what's not in the report."

"Excuse me?"

"Your thoughts. Your gut feeling," The Chief of Police explained.

Derrick cleared his throat, "Well Sir, Jo mentioned she had a sister who wanted to be a cop. There was something about that statement that didn't add up, so I did some digging. I visited the institution but of course, confidentiality meant they weren't going to tell me anything without a warrant, but I found a nurse who was willing to talk to me off the record. She told me about a patient named Jillian."

The Chief listened intently, unable to mask his concern.

"I showed her our class graduation photo and she pointed to Jo and said that she was Jillian. They were twins. Jo... the real Jo, visited her sister Jillian often. When she told her that she joined the academy, Jillian felt betrayed and killed her. No one suspected anything when a nurse went in to tell her that visiting hours were over, she was sitting on the floor crying... her sister had hung herself."

"So... what you are saying...?" The Chief of Police started to say.

"Is that Jo walked into the hospital, but Jillian walked out. In the confusion of a patient hanging themself, no one thought to check that the right sister was walking out of the institution."

"That explains how she escaped," the Chief of Police stated matter-of-factly, "but there is no way a mental patient could get past our psych tests... or the lie detector."

"I agree," Derrick answered, "and that had me stumped at first too. So I did some more digging and discovered that Jo, the real Jo, had applied to the academy the previous year. She passed all the tests except the P.A.R.E. So when she came back the following year, they gave her the physical test first. When she passed it, they did not get her to go through the rest of the tests again. They naturally assumed she didn't get dumber within the last year. They should have at least given her the lie detector test again, but since she passed it with flying colours the first time through, I'm guessing they assumed she didn't suddenly go rogue."

"And that allowed her to get into the academy under her sister's identity."

"Exactly," Derrick replied.

"So what you're saying Officer Stone, is that we trained this psycho to be a better cop killer?"

Derrick looked at the floor, then back to the Chief of Police. "That's exactly what I'm saying... Sir."

The Chief of Police stared at Derrick for a long time without saying a word. He opened his desk drawer then looked at Derrick.

"Since you know her better than anyone Officer Stone, I am

placing you in charge of finding this maniac and bringing her in. Dead or alive, I don't really care which, just find her and put an end to this, or a lot more cops are going to die. Do you have a problem with that?"

Images of Clay, Big Jim, and the thought of everyone she killed flashed through Derricks' mind.

"No problem at all. Sir."

"Good," the Chief of Police pulled a gold badge from the drawer and laid it on the desk in front of Derrick. "Then consider this your first assignment... Detective Stone."

As if on cue, Derrick's cell phone rang.

"It's her," Derrick said as he pressed the answer call button.

"Good morning, Sweety. How's my favourite cop doing these days?"

"Cut the shit Jo... or should I call you Jillian?"

"I'm impressed Sweety... very impressed. Did our wonderful Chief of Police put you in charge of bringing me in?"

Derrick did not reply.

"I take your silence as a yes. Then I guess the manhunt... I always hated that term, it's so sexist. But whatever, you'll be spending your sleepless nights trying to figure out where I am."

"I will find you," Derrick hissed into the phone.

"Of course you will Sweety, just not today. Well, I guess I should run. Run, did you get it? Manhunt... run."

Derrick said nothing.

"Oh pooh, so serious. Oh well, before I hang up, I need you to do one small thing for me, then we can play good cop, bad cop."

"And what would that be, Jillian?"

"Say goodbye to Daddy for mc."

The line went dead.

Derrick looked at the Chief of Police.

"You're their father?" It was more of a statement than a question. "That means you're the one who abused---"

Before Derrick could finish his sentence, the window shattered and the Chief's head jolted backwards.

Derrick dropped to the floor. He crawled to the window then cautiously looked out. On a rooftop across the street, Jillian stood up and casually flung a sniper rifle over her shoulder.

Derrick watched as she waved and blew him a kiss, then disappeared across the rooftops.

The Chief's secretary raced into the office and screamed at the sight of the dead Chief of Police. Derrick thumbed his radio to call in the murder, and the last known location of the sniper, even though he knew she was already long gone. He stood as other officers ran into the room.

Derrick grabbed the Detective's badge off the desk and left the office, and said to himself...

"Now we get to see what we're really made of."

~ The End ~

This page intentionally left blank

Crawford House Publishing

www.kenncrawford.com

www.ingramcontent.com/pod-product-compliance
Lightning Source LLC
Chambersburg PA
CBHW051952170626
46808CB00007B/2587